LOVE AND DARKNESS

A Novel by Marcus Ivy

Staten House

First Edition

Printed in the United States of America

ISBN: 979-8-89965-325-4

Cover design by: Marcus Ivy

Published by: Staten House

Cleveland, Ohio

I once believed love was the safest place a person could rest.

That it could heal what was broken. That it was light in the dark.

But love, I learned, can be the most dangerous lie of all.

It hides sharp teeth behind soft smiles.

It waits with open arms and closed hands.

And sometimes, it doesn't save you.

Sometimes—it burns you alive.

This is not a love story.

This is the truth I paid for in blood.

—E.H.

Chapter One:

A Heart's Hunger

Ever since she was a child, Elara dreamed of love. The kind of love whispered about in novels and seen in old films—passionate, magnetic, and unbreakable. Growing up in a small town in Vermont, she always felt like an outsider peering into a life that wasn't hers. She watched her friends marry their high school sweethearts while she chased career dreams in Boston and returned home for holidays to find herself seated at the kids' table, still single.

Now thirty-one, Elara had it all—or so it seemed. A cozy bookstore she owned in a picturesque town, a loyal golden retriever named Tilly, and a quaint cottage with ivy crawling up the walls. Her days passed in a comforting rhythm: opening the store with a steaming cup of coffee in hand, chatting with regulars about literature, walking Tilly through the maple-dotted trails, and curling up with a book each night. On the surface, she had curated a peaceful life.

But loneliness, she found, had a clever way of echoing through even the most charming spaces.

Her customers often commented on her smile, how warm and welcoming she was. They didn't see the ache underneath. They didn't see her linger by the window late into the night, watching couples walk hand in hand under streetlamps. Or the way she rearranged the romance section of her shop more often than necessary, as if doing so would invite her own story to begin.

Elara had dated over the years. Brief relationships that fizzled out, or promising beginnings that unraveled with time. No one had ever stayed. Some said she was too idealistic, too wrapped up in fairy tales. Others simply didn't see her the way she yearned to be seen.

And though she never said it aloud, Elara feared something deeper: that maybe she wasn't meant for love at all. Maybe she had been born to observe it in others, to write about it in her journal, but never to fully grasp it for herself.

She had just finished restocking a shelf when the bell over the bookstore door chimed. The storm outside had started only minutes ago, sheets of rain pouring from a suddenly angry sky. She expected a regular seeking shelter or a late-night reader with an umbrella dripping on the welcome mat.

Instead, a stranger stepped inside.

Tall. Lean. Drenched in rain but strangely composed. He removed his coat with care, revealing a tailored black sweater and dark jeans. He moved like someone who owned every room he entered but didn't feel the need to prove it.

"Looking for anything in particular?" Elara asked, her voice calm despite the pulse quickening in her chest.

"Yes," he said, meeting her gaze. His eyes were dark and sharp, as though they saw things others missed. "A book on rare poisonous plants."

She blinked.

"That's... specific," she said, trying not to sound unnerved.

He smiled faintly. "I've always found them fascinating. The elegance of danger."

She led him to the science section, watching him out of the corner of her eye as he scanned the shelves with purpose. She tried to guess his story—botanist? Academic? Writer of macabre fiction?

But he offered no further explanation.

"I'm Elara," she said, holding out her hand.

He hesitated a beat before taking it. "Damien."

And in that moment, though she didn't understand it yet, something shifted. A thread had been pulled. A door cracked open.

Elara didn't know that by the time she discovered who Damien really was, it would be too late.

But for now, all she felt was a flicker of something she hadn't felt in years.

Hope.

Chapter Two:

The Stranger

He appeared on a rainy Thursday. Damien Caldwell. His name alone echoed in Elara's thoughts long after he left her store that first night. There was something about him that didn't fit—a strange harmony of gentleness and distance, of warmth and something unreadable beneath the surface.

The next morning, she found herself reorganizing the botany section, running her fingers over the spines of titles she hadn't touched in months. It was absurd, she told herself, to think he might return so soon.

But he did. Two days later.

This time, he brought coffee. Black for him. Almond milk and cinnamon for her. "I figured I owed you for the help," he said, handing it to her with a small, almost reluctant smile.

And then he stayed.

Not long—twenty minutes, maybe. Just enough to ask about her favorite books, to mention his own interest in ancient herbal remedies and folklore, to leave her wondering what shadows lingered behind his eyes.

Over the following weeks, his visits became a pattern. Every few days. Always in the late afternoon. Sometimes with coffee, sometimes a book recommendation, once even a small bouquet of forget-me-nots.

Each time, they talked a little more. About literature, local history, the strange architecture of his family's estate on the edge of town. He listened when she spoke, genuinely listened, and offered reflections that startled her with their insight.

Still, he was careful—measured. He shared just enough to keep her interested, never enough to truly understand him. There were no stories of childhood mischief, no mentions of old friends. His words were filtered, wrapped in charm and subtle detachment.

The town began to notice. Mrs. Galloway, who ran the antique shop next door, asked if Elara was seeing someone. Her friend Becca raised an eyebrow when she saw them laughing by the register.

And Elara, against her better judgment, let herself hope.

One afternoon, Damien offered to help her carry boxes of used books from the storage unit behind the shop. As they worked side by side, sweat and laughter mixing, she noticed the small things: the way he moved with quiet precision, the care he took not to let a single book fall.

They finished just as the sun began to dip below the hills.

"Dinner?" he asked casually, as if it were the most natural thing in the world.

She hesitated. Then nodded.

They ate at a tiny bistro tucked away behind the main street. Candlelight danced between them, illuminating the corners of his face she hadn't yet mapped. He spoke of travel—briefly. Paris. A monastery in Romania. A jungle trek in South America. But his stories were strange, abstract, almost dreamlike.

And then, as the night wore on, something shifted. He asked if she believed people could be inherently evil.

Elara paused, caught off guard. "I think people can be shaped by their pasts," she said. "But everyone has a choice."

Damien didn't respond immediately. He looked at her in a way that made her heart stutter.

"I think some people are born into darkness," he said softly. "And some spend their lives trying to escape it."

She didn't know what to say. The moment passed quickly, replaced by laughter and casual conversation.

But that night, lying awake in bed, Elara couldn't shake the feeling that she'd been invited to glimpse something hidden—something fragile and terrifying.

She told herself not to read into it. That he was just complicated. That maybe, finally, she had found someone who saw the world the way she did.

What she didn't know was that Damien had already chosen her.

Not as a lover.

As something else entirely.

Chapter Three:

The Invitation

The invitation arrived on thick, cream-colored parchment sealed with red wax. Elara found it tucked inside the latest botanical book Damien had gifted her—The Language of Poison. She flipped to the inside cover and the envelope fell out, bearing her name in elegant script.

She hesitated before breaking the seal. Inside was a single card:

You're invited to an evening gathering at Ashthorne Manor. Saturday at 8 p.m. — D

Ashthorne Manor.

The name alone conjured images of gothic halls and candlelit corridors. Locals spoke of the Caldwell estate in hushed tones—rumors of tragedies, secretive family rituals, and land cursed with sorrow. Few had ever seen its interior, and fewer still had been welcomed in.

Her first instinct was to decline.

But curiosity, mingled with the pull Damien had over her, won out.

Saturday came quickly. Elara stood before the mirror, adjusting the velvet ribbon at her neck. She wore a deep green dress, simple yet elegant. Tilly whined softly as she reached for her coat, and Elara knelt to stroke her fur.

"I'll be home soon," she promised.

The drive to Ashthorne Manor wound through dense forest and fog. Her phone lost signal ten minutes into the journey. The road narrowed, flanked by ancient trees and gnarled branches. Just when she considered turning back, the manor appeared—monolithic and shadowed in twilight.

A wrought iron gate creaked open at her arrival. The manor's facade loomed like a relic of another age, its windows aglow with soft amber light. A man in dark formalwear greeted her at the door, offering no introduction as he ushered her inside.

The foyer took her breath away—marble floors, grand staircases, portraits that seemed to watch her. Guests milled about in elegant attire, their laughter restrained, their smiles brittle.

Damien found her near the fireplace. He looked striking in a dark suit, his eyes gleaming with something unreadable.

"I'm glad you came," he said.

"You didn't tell me this would be a... ball?" she asked, glancing around.

"Not quite. It's a tradition," Damien said. "My family hosts it once a year. To remember who we are."

He didn't elaborate.

They danced. Slowly, deliberately. A waltz echoing through the vast hall. Elara felt like she was floating through a dream—or a warning. She asked questions, but Damien deflected them with charm and veiled answers. Every so often, she caught a strange look from one of the other guests. Some whispered as she passed.

By the third dance, she'd had enough.

"Can we step outside?" she asked.

Damien nodded and led her through a glass door to the garden. The air was cold, heavy with the scent of lavender and something metallic.

"I've never met your family," she said. "Who are all these people?"

"They're part of something old," Damien said, voice lower now. "Something that doesn't belong to this world anymore."

She frowned. "Damien, you're scaring me."

He turned to her, his expression unreadable. "I never wanted to. I wanted you to see the beauty in it first."

"In what?" she asked.

He took her hand.

"In the darkness."

A sound broke the tension—the cry of a woman, distant yet piercing, quickly muffled. Elara froze.

"What was that?"

Damien didn't answer.

Suddenly, hands closed around her arms. Two men emerged from the shadows, dressed like the others but with no pretense of politeness.

"Damien!" she cried.

"I'm sorry," he said. "But you have to understand. You were chosen."

She struggled as they dragged her through a side door, down a stone staircase, and into a narrow, candlelit corridor. The air grew colder, more suffocating. She screamed, kicked, begged—but no one came.

At the end of the hall was a heavy wooden door.

Behind it, a room.

Stone walls. Iron chains bolted to the bed.

And silence.

They left her there. The lock clicked behind them.

Elara sobbed, shaking, trying to make sense of what had happened. Hours passed. The candles burned low. Then, in the distance, she heard it again:

A scream.

Muffled. Terrified. Female.

She wasn't alone.

And whatever Ashthorne Manor truly was, it was far more monstrous than she could've imagined.

Chapter Four:

Behind Locked Doors

Time blurred in the cold stone room. Elara had no idea how long she'd been there—hours, days, or something in between. The air was damp, stale with the scent of mildew and rust. Chains bit into her wrists where they connected her to the wrought-iron bedframe. Her dress was torn from the struggle, her skin bruised, but her spirit was still intact.

She hadn't given them the satisfaction of breaking.

Occasionally, a tray of food would be slid through a small opening in the door. Sometimes, the water came laced with a bitter aftertaste, and she learned quickly to ration what seemed clean. Voices echoed through the stone hallways beyond her cell. Male, female. Some laughing. Some whispering. One night, she heard crying. It wasn't hers.

And then came the screams.

They weren't constant. That made them worse. They came at unpredictable hours—long, drawn-out howls of pure terror, always muffled, always silenced too soon. Elara pressed her hands over her ears and whispered to herself, trying to drown them out with remembered pages of her favorite novels. But the screams lingered. They curled around her like smoke, seeping into her dreams.

Then one morning—or night, she couldn't tell—the key turned in the door. It creaked open, and a woman entered. Tall, red-haired, dressed in crimson satin. Her heels clicked against the stone as she approached, her green eyes curious.

"You must be Elara," she said, with a voice like velvet over broken glass. "I'm Maren. Damien's sister."

Elara glared at her. "Let me go."

Maren smiled faintly, perching on the edge of the bed like they were chatting over tea. "I'm afraid it's not that simple. You've been... chosen. You're part of something bigger now."

"I don't want to be."

"That's not up to you."

Elara yanked at her chains. "What do you people want?"

Maren leaned in, her eyes glittering. "To survive. To endure. To keep our legacy alive. And you, sweet thing, are the perfect vessel."

Before Elara could reply, Maren pressed something cold and sharp to her throat—a silver talisman etched with strange runes. Elara flinched.

"You feel it, don't you?" Maren whispered. "The pull?"

"I feel revulsion," Elara spat.

Maren chuckled. "You will see. It changes you. Damien tried to spare you, you know. He thought you might join us willingly. He's always been the soft one."

With that, she rose and swept out of the room, leaving Elara in silence once more.

Time passed.

Then, the sound she'd longed for.

A voice. A knock. A familiar cry.

"Elara?"

Her sister.

"Lina!" Elara screamed, struggling upright. "I'm here! I'm—"

A scream.

Not Elara's this time.

Lina's voice rose sharply in terror, cut off in a heartbeat.

"No!" Elara sobbed. "No, please, don't hurt her—please!"

But silence returned. Heavier than ever.

Elara sank to the floor, shaking. Guilt and fury warred within her. They had lured her sister. Her family was looking for her—and now they might suffer for it.

She couldn't let that happen.

Something inside her cracked, and then hardened. The tears dried. Her breathing steadied. She stared at the chains on her wrists, then at the door.

They wanted her to surrender.

But Elara was no longer waiting to be rescued.

She was planning her escape.

Even if she had to bleed to get it.

Even if it meant dragging every one of the Caldwells into the light.

Starting with Damien.

Chapter Five:

Whispers in the Walls

Elara stopped marking time in days and instead counted by the screams.

Each one etched a tally in her mind, more vivid than any clock or calendar. The manor's silence between them was deceptive, a thick fog of dread that crept in and filled her lungs. But that silence had begun to speak.

In the quiet hours, when no one came, Elara pressed her ear to the stone wall beside her bed. She heard things— soft shifting, whispers muffled by stone. At first, she thought it was the manor breathing. Then she realized they were voices.

Some were unintelligible. Others too faint. But one night, a clear phrase cut through the silence: "North wall. Count the stones."

Elara jolted upright.

Her fingers flew over the stones in the north wall. She counted. Twenty-three rows high, fifteen across. One, two, three—until her fingertips brushed a stone colder than the others. Slightly loose.

With effort and torn fingernails, she worked it free. Behind it, a hollow space. Inside—a folded paper and a small, rusted key.

The paper was faded, words scribbled hastily:

"They see everything but feel nothing. The tunnels lead to the old well. Do not trust the silence."

Elara's heart raced. It wasn't just her. Someone else had been here. Maybe still was.

The next morning, Damien entered.

He looked tired. Worn. His clothes immaculate, but his eyes clouded. He set down a tray of fruit and bread, eyes flicking to her wrists.

"You haven't eaten in two days."

"I'm not hungry," Elara said, flatly.

"You'll need your strength."

"For what?" she snapped.

He hesitated. "For what's coming."

She stood slowly. "You're still pretending you care?"

"I do care." His voice was soft. "You don't understand. My family... I was born into this. You weren't supposed to be a part of it."

"And yet here I am."

Damien stepped closer. "Maren is watching. She knows something's... changing. You're changing."

He reached into his coat and placed something in her palm. A thin, copper pendant shaped like a crescent moon.

"She won't recognize this. Wear it. It might buy you time."

"Time for what?"

He didn't answer. He left.

Later that night, Elara began scratching at the mortar behind the loose stone. The key didn't fit her chains—but maybe it belonged to a door, or a tunnel.

Then came the voice again. Not from the wall, but from the other side of the door.

"Is someone there?" a hoarse whisper asked.

Elara froze. "Yes. Who are you?"

"Name's Sophia," the voice replied. "Been here months. Maybe longer. You're the first new one I've heard in a while."

"Do you know the way out?"

Silence.

"I know pieces. But not all. They take us through the tunnel sometimes. Sedated."

"Can you help me find it?"

"If you help me too."

Elara nodded to the darkness. "Then we start tonight."

From the other side, a soft laugh. Bitter. "Welcome to Ashthorne Manor."

Chapter Six:

The Others

The voice behind the wall became Elara's only anchor to sanity.

Sophia spoke in fragments, often interrupted by waves of paranoia or fatigue, but Elara pieced her story together over whispered conversations. She'd been taken from a university campus two towns over. Like Elara, she had once believed Damien was a rescuer, not a hunter.

"They keep the women they think are 'pure enough,'" Sophia had said bitterly. "The others don't survive the first week."

Elara kept the pendant Damien gave her hidden beneath her blouse. Maren hadn't returned, but her presence lingered like perfume soaked into the walls. Elara knew she was being watched—perhaps even tested.

The tunnel passage behind the north wall was too narrow to fit through yet. She'd need tools, strength, and time.

But time was thinning.

That evening, the door creaked again. Two men entered, dragging a girl between them—barely conscious, her limbs limp. They didn't speak to Elara, but the message was clear.

Another one.

They laid her on the floor, and left.

Elara scrambled to her side. The girl had a split lip and bruised arms. She stirred.

"Hey. It's okay," Elara whispered.

"W-Where am I?" the girl croaked.

"You're not alone."

Elara cleaned her wounds with water from the tray. She was barely older than Lina.

Later that night, Sophia whispered urgently. "They're preparing for a ritual."

Elara stiffened. "When?"

"Soon. The Blood Moon. They do something terrible every time it rises."

"What happens?"

"Girls vanish. And we hear screaming from the altar room below the chapel. No one ever returns."

Fear wrapped itself around Elara's spine like a serpent. She looked at the girl sleeping beside her. She had to act.

But before she could plan her next move, she heard something impossible.

A knock.

Then a voice.

"Elara!"

Her heart stopped. Lina.

"Lina!" Elara ran to the door, shouting. "I'm here! Lina!"

A shriek. Then silence.

The next day, Damien appeared with blood on his collar.

"You brought her here?" Elara demanded, trembling.

"She came," he said quietly. "I tried to keep her away."

"What did they do to her?"

"She's alive. But for how long... I don't know."

He stepped closer.

"You want to escape?" he asked.

She didn't reply. Her silence was answer enough.

"Then meet me tomorrow. Midnight. If you're sure."

And then he was gone.

Sophia's whisper came an hour later.

"He's lying, Elara."

"I know," she whispered back. "But I need him to believe I believe him."

Outside the walls, Ashthorne Manor stirred. The Blood Moon was rising.

Chapter Seven:

The Legacy Revealed

Elara hadn't slept. Not truly. Between whispered warnings from Sophia, the unconscious girl beside her, and the memory of Lina's voice at the door, she felt her body running on nothing but instinct and defiance.

The pendant Damien gave her hung cold at her throat. She didn't trust him. Not anymore. But she would use him as long as it bought her time.

That evening, two silent women arrived at her door. Their faces were painted with symbols, their eyes dull and unfeeling. They said nothing, only beckoned.

Elara followed.

They led her through a spiral hallway beneath the manor—walls of polished stone carved with glyphs she couldn't understand. She passed cells. Empty ones. But she felt them echo with pain. As they reached a circular chamber, a chill ran down her spine.

Maren waited.

Draped in a crimson robe, she stood at an altar of black stone. Behind her, a circular skylight revealed the waxing blood moon, red and growing.

"You must be frightened," Maren said.

Elara kept her mouth shut.

"You should be."

Maren stepped forward, her voice low and reverent. "Once every generation, when the moon bleeds and the veil thins, we offer the blood of those who carry the Ember Vein. Most burn. Some bless us. But only once... has the Flame tried to awaken."

Elara flinched. "What are you talking about?"

"Your ancestor," Maren said smoothly. "She fled from this house. Took her power with her. But the Ember Vein survived. Through your mother. Through you."

"No," Elara whispered. "That's not possible."

"Oh, but it is. You think your family left all this behind? No, my dear. They buried it. Tried to forget. But power like this never forgets."

Elara's fists clenched. "You want to use me."

Maren smiled. "No, Elara. I want to crown you."

Lightning cracked outside. The torches flared unnaturally.

"If you survive the Rite, the Root Flame will awaken beneath this house. You will have a choice: burn us all and become a god... or rule in my place."

Elara stepped back. "You're insane."

"Or perhaps I am simply the one who remembers."

Maren raised her hand. From a hidden alcove, an ancient tome floated toward her—its pages breathing with a life of their own.

"You were never looking for love," Maren said. "You were searching for purpose. Now you have it."

Elara turned, heart thundering, as the blood moon climbed higher.

Chapter Eight:

Fractures

Elara paced her room, the echo of Maren's words still pounding in her mind. *Become a god. Rule. Or burn them all.*

Sophia whispered through the wall again. "It's close. The ritual. They're preparing the chapel. I can smell the oils."

Elara pressed her forehead against the cold stone. "Maren said I could survive it. That I might be... the one."

A long pause. Then: "Then they'll never let you leave."

A key rattled in the door.

It opened. Damien stood in the threshold. His eyes were sunken. His hands bloodstained. He was breathing heavily, like he'd run to her.

"I need to show you something."

She didn't trust him, but nodded. He led her through a side corridor lit only by dying sconces. Down a spiral of stone, past old paintings covered in cloth. Then through a narrow door into a hidden room beneath the library.

Inside: Lina.

She was pale, weak—but alive. Chained at the wrist, slumped against the wall. There were bruises on her collarbone, dried blood at her temple. But she stirred at the sound of Elara's gasp.

"Elara?" Lina's voice cracked like ice.

Elara dropped beside her, holding her sister's face. "I'm here. I'm going to get you out."

Tears stung her eyes. Guilt surged like a flood. "I'm so sorry. I didn't know they'd hurt you."

"They said you were one of them," Lina whispered. "That you'd chosen this."

"I didn't," Elara said fiercely. "I would never."

Damien stood a few paces back, silent.

"They spared her—for you," he said eventually. "Maren wants you emotionally bound. Pain fuels the rite. The deeper the wound, the stronger the flame."

"You let them do this?" Elara turned on him, fury bursting through her voice.

"I didn't know. Not until it was too late. But I've stolen the key. You have tonight. After the moon reaches its peak, they'll take you both to the altar."

He tossed her a small iron key. It clattered on the stone floor.

"Why are you helping me now?" she asked.

His expression was hollow. "Because I thought I was born into something divine. I thought this family was chosen. But now I know we're a curse. And if anyone can end it... it's you."

She didn't thank him. She only nodded. Her mind was already planning.

Later that night, Elara knelt near the wall where Sophia's voice always came. She whispered the plan. Sophia would guide her through the crypt tunnels—part of the old foundation of Ashthorne Manor. They ran beneath the gardens and, if legend was true, out into the woods.

"There's a grate in the chapel's southern wall," Sophia murmured. "That's your exit. But it's guarded."

"Can you distract them?"

"I've been here longer than you can imagine. I know the pressure points. I'll get them looking the other way."

They mapped it in murmurs—every turn, every danger. Time was thin.

Elara returned to Lina, unlocked her chain, and wrapped her sister in a thick wool cloak from the bed. "We're getting out," she whispered. "I swear it."

The manor groaned above them.

Torches were lit in ceremonial rows. The great bells began to chime—deep, discordant.

And outside the manor, the Blood Moon rose fully—drenching the sky in crimson.

Deep beneath the house, something old and buried stirred.

The Root Flame had begun to wake.

Chapter Nine:

Embers in the Dark

The tunnel air was thick with dust and rot. Elara half-carried, half-dragged Lina through the crumbling passage, each step a test of will. Behind them, the distant toll of bells counted down the final hour.

Sophia's voice guided from the shadows. "Left at the arch. There's a loose stone—step over it."

Every turn felt like a maze deeper into the bones of the manor. The crypt walls were lined with urns and bones, some marked with runes Elara didn't recognize. The smell of blood was faint but constant.

Lina coughed. "How much farther?"

"Close," Elara whispered. "Just hold on."

They reached a stone alcove where a rusted iron grate blocked the tunnel's end. It was smaller than expected—no more than three feet tall—but behind it, moonlight gleamed.

Sophia appeared, cloak fluttering as if moved by wind that wasn't there. Her eyes locked with Elara's.

"I've drawn two of the acolytes away. You have five minutes before they check the grounds."

Elara turned to Lina. "Can you crawl?"

Lina nodded, shakily.

She pushed Lina through the grate first, heart pounding. Then followed, her shoulders scraping against the stone. On the other side, wild brambles snagged at their clothes, but it was real—the woods.

The manor loomed behind them like a wound against the red sky.

Then, a scream.

Sophia.

Elara turned back. "No!"

From the shadows of the crypt, a figure emerged. Maren. Her robes billowed with unnatural force, and her eyes glowed faintly red.

"You disappoint me," she said, voice echoing.

Elara shoved Lina behind her.

"You're not going to stop me."

"I'm not here to stop you," Maren said, stepping closer. "I'm here to offer you a final truth."

She raised her hand. A memory burned through Elara's mind—her mother in the hospital, whispering a name. A name Elara never understood. *Seraphine*.

"She was the last to awaken the Flame. Your blood carries her burden. And her choice."

Elara staggered.

"You can still join us," Maren said softly. "Take your place at the altar. Or run—and doom your sister to carry it instead."

The moon above pulsed.

Elara's fists clenched. "I won't let you rewrite our fate."

She turned. Grabbed Lina's hand. And ran.

Behind them, Maren's voice echoed like prophecy.

"You can run from the manor... but not from what's in your blood."

The night closed around them, and the flame within Elara began to burn.

Chapter Ten:

The Heart of Ashthorne

The chapel pulsed with the sick light of the Blood Moon, its windows casting red veins across the cracked marble floor. Cloaked figures chanted in unison, their voices melding into a low, hungry vibration that shook the very stones.

Elara stood among them, cloaked in the robes of the fallen acolyte. Her heart thundered. She'd left Lina hidden in the woods near the old cottage ruins—but now, one of the cultists dragged a limp form to the altar.

Her breath caught.

Lina.

Her sister's wrists were bound in red leather, eyes glassy, barely conscious. Her skin was glowing faintly, threaded with pulsing lines of ember.

"No..." Elara whispered.

A voice rang out above the chant. "The Flame has chosen."

Maren stepped into the light, her robe discarded to reveal the ritualist armor beneath—bones sewn into silk, red ash streaked across her face. Her eyes locked with Elara's.

"You were always meant to awaken her, not become her," she said. "The Flame never lies."

Before Elara could move, hands seized her. She was dragged forward and thrown to the floor beside the altar, forced to watch as the flame beneath the chapel—a pit of smoldering red, laced with whispering tendrils—began to open like a mouth.

Lina stirred. Her lips parted. A single word escaped: "Elara..."

Then—

Screams.

From the pit below, twisted faces rose within the fire. Familiar. Tortured. Sophia. Seraphine. Her mother.

"You see them," Maren said, her voice velvet with venom. "Every woman whose blood fed the Flame. Including your own bloodline. Including me."

Elara's eyes widened.

"I am Seraphine's twin," Maren said, stepping closer. "She chose martyrdom. I chose power. And I've waited generations to finish what we began."

Elara struggled, but the cultists held fast. The Ember Vein in Lina's chest flared—burning through her veins, lifting her from the stone. She began to scream.

"Stop!" Elara sobbed. "Take me instead!"

"No," Maren whispered. "You're the gate. She is the flame."

Suddenly—a crash.

Damien.

He staggered through the chapel doors, blood-soaked, dragging the dying body of a robed elder. In his free hand, he held a black blade—etched in silver.

"The Blade of Withering," he said hoarsely. "It severs the Flame's claim."

The chanting faltered. Several cultists turned, but Maren raised her hand and they resumed, louder. The floor trembled.

Elara looked up at him, then at Lina, then at the faces in the fire.

"I'm not the gate," she whispered. "I'm the lock."

She ripped free of her captors, pain lancing through her arm where a clawed hand tore flesh. Staggering to Damien, she grabbed the blade. He tried to stop her.

"Elara—"

"There's no other way."

She turned the blade on herself.

It slid into her side. Not flesh alone—it passed into something deeper. The Ember Vein flared. The pit howled. Screams from a thousand voices filled the chamber.

The Flame recoiled, the faces within it shrieking, stretching into light. Maren screamed as her body began to burn from the inside out, ash spilling from her mouth.

Lina fell to the ground, unconscious. Damien threw himself over her, shielding her from the falling debris.

Elara stood amid the storm of fire and bone, her form glowing gold and red, her eyes hollow with flame. She turned her face to the pit and whispered a final word:

"Remember."

The chapel exploded. Walls folded in. The ceiling cracked like eggshell. Fire poured upward like breath from a dead god.

Damien crawled out of the rubble with Lina in his arms. The manor behind him collapsed inward, consumed by roots and flame and silence.

There was no scream. Only light—and then nothing.

Ashthorne was gone.

Epilogue:

The Watcher in the Woods

One year later.

Spring had come early to Greystone Valley. The forest no longer wept ash, and the birds had returned to the trees. But Elara's cottage, now Lina's, stood quieter than it ever had.

Inside, the air smelled of paint and dried flowers. The walls were lined with portraits—each one a different vision of Elara. In some, she was serene, her eyes closed in peace. In others, fierce and aflame, her gaze a challenge to gods.

Lina stood at the easel, brush trembling in her hand. She never painted the same image twice. But every version she created carried the same heartache: the shape of a sister lost, the ghost of a woman who had given everything.

Damien appeared in the doorway, a basket of wild herbs in one hand. "You didn't sleep again."

"I dreamed of the chapel," Lina whispered. "But it was still burning."

He crossed the room, setting the basket down beside her. "Dreams fade. This—" he gestured to the room, to her paintings, "—this is how we remember."

Outside, the wind shifted.

Lina stepped onto the porch. The woods stood silent, dappled in green and gold. But something moved between the trees—a figure barely glimpsed. A deer, tall and lean.

Its eyes glowed faintly red.

Lina froze.

A whisper rode the wind, curling around her ear like smoke:

"Remember."

She turned back inside and closed the door. But for a moment, the paintings on the wall flickered—one of them now showed Elara standing not in fire, but beneath a blood-red tree, smiling.

The forest kept its secrets.

And something—someone—still watched from the dark.

www.ingramcontent.com/pod-product-compliance
Lightning Source LLC
Chambersburg PA
CBHW070825260626
47161CB00006B/2409